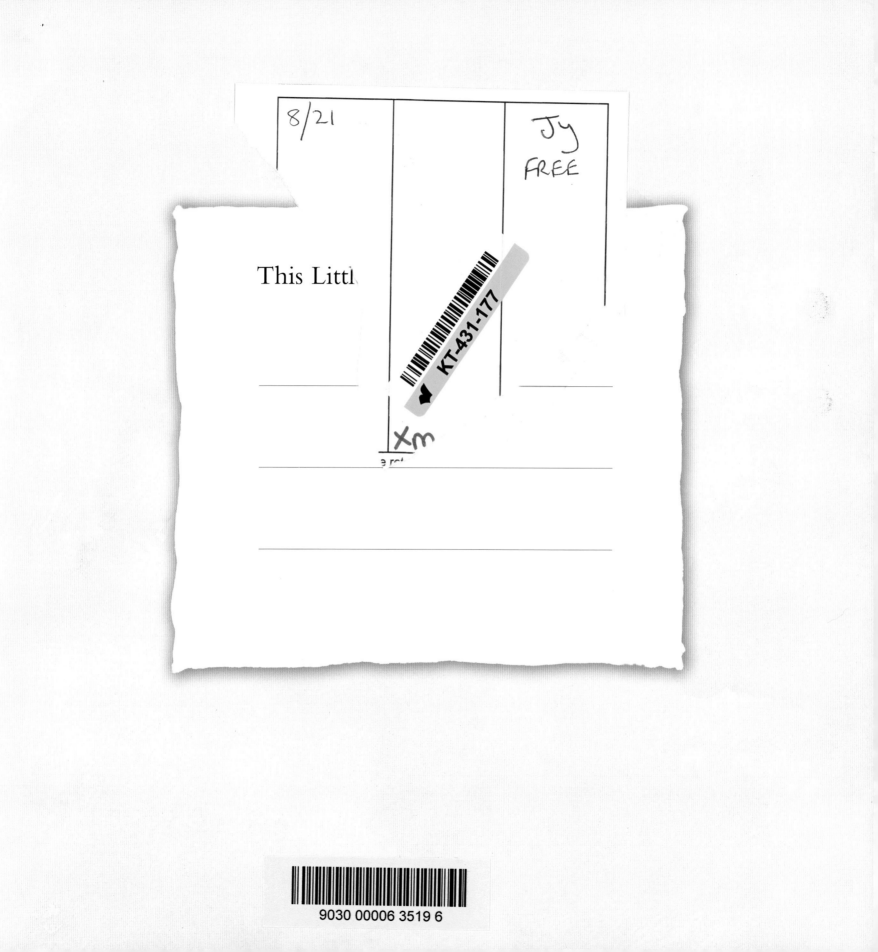

8/21

Jy
FREE

This Littl

KT-431-177

Xm

With thanks to Banyan and Dogwood classes

of Brackenbury Primary School 2009

for all their wonderful ideas.

LITTLE TIGER PRESS LTD,
an imprint of the Little Tiger Group
1 Coda Studios, 189 Munster Road, London SW6 6AW
www.littletiger.co.uk

First published in Great Britain 2010
This edition published 2011

A CIP catalogue record for this book is available from the British Library

Printed in China

LTP/1900/2351/0718

2 4 6 8 10 9 7 5 3

Ten Christmas Wishes

Claire Freedman   Gail Yerrill

LITTLE TIGER
LONDON

One shining Christmas star
Is lighting up the sky.
Make a wish now, Little Mouse,
On that star up high.

Little Mouse is wishing hard,
"Oh let it snow tonight,
So when I wake tomorrow,
The world is sparkling white!"

Look! A second Christmas star,
Together they make two.
Little Rabbit, this new wish
Is waiting just for you.

Little Rabbit makes his wish:
"A scarf that never ends!
To wrap around me warm and snug,
And also round my friends!"

See another dazzling star,
Let's count them, one, two, three!
Little Squirrel, make your wish,
Now what will that wish be?

"I wish, I wish," says Squirrel,
"That my family far away
Would come to stay for Christmas,
And arrive right now — today!"

Another star is glittering,
So now you can see four.
This is Little Hedgehog's star,
Now what will she wish for?

Little Hedgehog wishes for
The best Christmas tree ever,
With branches reaching up so high,
They seem to stretch forever!

Five stars in the velvet sky,
All twinkling silver-bright.
Little Bear, one shines for you,
So make your wish tonight.

"I wish for lots of presents,
For all my friends to share,
The label on the biggest gift
Would read 'To Little Bear'!"

One more silver star shines bright,
Six stars now light the sky.
Rabbit makes his Christmas wish
Upon his star up high.

"I wish I had a snowball,
A great big GIANT one,
My friends could help me roll it,
We'd all have so much fun!"

Another star is peeping,
So seven stars shine bright.
This new star glows for Little Mouse,
What will she wish tonight?

Little Mouse is wishing for
A pie all warm and sweet,
The biggest, best pie ever,
That's so **wonderful** to eat!

The midnight sky is shimmering,
Eight Christmas stars now shine,
"My turn to wish," says Little Bear,
"The newest star is mine!"

"I wish my mum would read me tales
Of Santa on his sleigh,
So while I'm curled up snug in bed,
I'll know he's on his way!"

toys

Nine Christmas stars all twinkle
So brightly from afar.
Little Badger, one's for you,
Come wish upon your star.

Little Badger can't sit still,
He cries, "I don't know how
I'll last a **moment** longer —
I wish Christmas time was NOW!"

Ten Christmas stars are shining bright,
The last star is for you,
So close your eyes and make a wish,
May all your dreams come true!

We wish you Christmas sparkle,
Like the starry skies above,
A time of joy and wonder,
And a Christmas filled with love.

More great books from Little Tiger Press!

When Will It Snow?
Kathryn White
Alison Edgson

Is It Christmas Yet?
Jane Chapman

Big Bear Little Bear
DAVID BEDFORD
JANE CHAPMAN

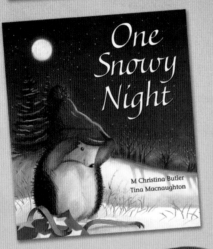

One Snowy Night
M Christina Butler
Tina Macnaughton

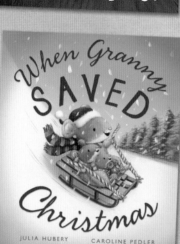

When Granny SAVED Christmas
JULIA HUBERY   CAROLINE PEDLER

I've Seen Santa!
David Bedford
Illustrated by
Tim Warnes

For information regarding any
of the above titles or for our catalogue,
please contact us:
Little Tiger Press, 1 Coda Studios,
189 Munster Road, London SW6 6AW
Tel: 020 7385 6333
E-mail: contact@littletiger.co.uk
www.littletiger.co.uk